The Rowdy R...

Our Cranky Crew

*words & pictures
by Natasha Oliver*

Dedicated to

Avery R. and Katelyn D.
whose imagination and excitement
truly helped me finish this book.
Thanks for the inspiration!

First paperback edition May 2021

ISBN 978-1734107845 (paperback edition)

Printed and bound in the United States of America
F4Bpublishing@fun4thebrain.com
Published by Tashilex Publishing
Maugansville, MD, 21740

Visit https://www. Fun4theBrain.com

Jasper Nathaniel Tobias Finnegan!!!

He peeked out from his hiding spot.
His mom called his name, not just one,
but all four!

He knew he must go, scared or not.

"I've put all the food Captain Fitz fancies there.
Even his pumpernickel bread.
I know that the pirates have seemed cranky today,
But don't frown, keep smiling instead."

As he walked down the hall Jasper
heard a weak squeak,
Cullen's head peaked out of his hole.

Lark whined, "I made them new clothes with their favorite colors, and I had to bring them all back!

The green shirt made Zed itch.
The red pants made Eve twitch.
And the boots, Riggs said,
"I want black."

The Captain and crew were so cranky, but WHY?

"Someone must have stolen their gold. I bet it's the cat, it has GOT to be her. Only THAT cat would be so bold."

We don't have a cat.

 The last time the crew was in THIS bad of a mood was when Captain lost his best hat.

The Captain then said, "We are now mean and grumpy. This is just how our crew should be.

I've read all the rules and to be
the best pirates,
We must change many things. You
will see."

"I found this old book buried in an old crate.
It belonged to Great Captain Stu.

It lists all the rules and guidelines and goals
He had for leading his crew."

"So, for pirates, our moods are too cheerful,
And also our clothes are too bright.

Donations to people who are NOT pirates

Most pirates all dress
in dark and drab colors,
It's there on page 2,
on the right."

They flipped through the book to see what it said. They read through each rule on each page.

Then Cullen asked Lark to add in one more, That said the cat must stay in a cage.

We don't have a cat.

It also says that to be a great pirate, you can't have a mouth that is clean,

WANTED

For piracy, and being scary and mean

Stinky Breath Sterling
$280

As breath that is stinky and teeth that are black,

Make pirates seem scary and mean.

I've asked for some boots in a
dull shade of grey,
And jackets as black as can be.

Our teeth will soon match as we're
no longer brushing.
Are holes showing yet, can you see?

Lark - age 2 - bunny leg

Lark - age 7 - crayon leg

Sebastian builds legs in all shapes and sizes. He even made one from a toy!

Lark - age 11 - painted flower leg

 Riggs plays kazoo music that makes us all dance.

We're not sure what's up with Roy.

We win awards
for our hair,
thanks to
Fred and Zed.

We've all
learned to read
from Eve.

I know you all want to be the **best** pirates, Some think that means mean and tough.

Crew needed!
MUST:

- Be mean
- Be tough
- Have black teeth
- Have bad breath
- Dress in drab colors
- Be grouchy

Other Crews

But, on the Rascal, we **aren't** like the others, Just being **ourselves** is enough.

Crew needed!
MUST:

- Work hard
- Be yourself!

Rowdy Rascal

You're right!
Each of you brings something unique that we need.
Together we make the best crew!
The new rule will say, each and every day,
Just try to be the best you.

We are the best pirates,
And we dress in bright colors.
We can be cheerful and we smile.

We are often quite rowdy,
We sing and we scowl,
And we do it all in style.

Be the Best You!

Always Be YOU!

Hi! I am Smiggles.
Can you go back
and find me on
each page?

Don't forget to leave your review on Amazon!

Natasha Oliver has been creating educational games for over a decade
and has now brought her heart for kids and learning to picture books!
There will be many more books and games to come.
Be sure to check out all the free educational games at www.fun4thebrain.com.

Made in the USA
Las Vegas, NV
20 August 2022

53506398R00021